The Helpful Puppy

by **Kim Zarins**

illustrated by

Emily Arnold McCully

Holiday House / New York

All the animals helped out at the farm—
all except the puppy.
"I want to help out too!"

He asked the rooster what to do.
The rooster crowed, "Each day
I *COCK-A-DOODLE-DO*
and wake everyone up."
"I can do that too," the puppy yipped.
"Let me help!"
But the puppy could only yelp.

Then the puppy saw the ox hauling a
heavy cart. He put his paws on a wheel.
"I can push the cart along!"
But he was wrong.

He watched the cat chasing a mouse.
The puppy barked, "I can do that too!"
"Nah," the cat said, "mice are too fast for you."

The puppy found the hens pecking at grain.
"How do you help on the farm?" he asked.
The chickens clucked, "We lay eggs!"

The puppy put his tail between his legs.

The puppy saw the horse in his stall.
"Could I carry people around?" the puppy asked.
The horse snickered, "You're a little small."

Then the puppy visited the cow.
The farmer squirted the milk into a pail.
"Can I make milk?" he asked.
The cow replied, "Of course not. You're a male."

Next the puppy saw some sheep and cheered.
"Yippee! I can give fur, like you give wool!"
"Na-ah-ah-ah," the sheep *baaed.*
"You'd look silly sheared."

The sheepdog hustled so the sheep wouldn't stray. "Can I help? Can I help?" the puppy whined.

"Not now," the sheepdog said.
"Someday."
But someday seemed so far away.

Then the puppy heard THE WHISTLE.
It quivered in his nose and in every limb.

He raced toward the sound because he knew
the whistle was just for him.

His boy was home from school.
It was time to play!

He jumped and licked and dashed
and wiggled for the rest of the day.

Under the blankets
the puppy snuggled with his boy,
and the boy hugged him tight.
Then the mother came in
to kiss her son good night.

The puppy's eyes were closed,
but he heard her voice above:
"Cows give milk and oxen pull.
Hens lay eggs and sheep give wool.
But only our puppy gives love."

To Arthur, with love—K. Z.

Text copyright © 2012 by Kim Zarins
Illustrations copyright © 2012 by Emily Arnold McCully
All Rights Reserved
HOLIDAY HOUSE is registered in the U.S. Patent and Trademark Office.
Printed and Bound in May 2012 at Kwong Fat Offset Printing Co., Ltd.,
Dongguan City, China.
The text typeface is Hank BT.
The artwork was created with watercolors.
www.holidayhouse.com
First Edition
1 3 5 7 9 10 8 6 4 2

Library of Congress Cataloging-in-Publication Data
Zarins, Kim.
The helpful puppy / by Kim Zarins ; illustrated by Emily Arnold McCully. — 1st ed.
p. cm.
Summary: A puppy who wants to help around the farm like all the other animals eventually learns exactly what his job is.
ISBN 978-0-8234-2318-7 (hardcover)
[1. Dogs—Fiction. 2. Domestic animals—Fiction. 3. Farm life—Fiction.] I. McCully, Emily Arnold, ill. II. Title.
PZ8.3.Z332He 2012
[E]—dc22
2010039541